4 WAR 5 TIME 6

my Forever

DRESS

by Harriet Ziefert

illustrated by Liz Murphy

🍎 Blue Apple Books

For my grandfather, a tailor, who hemmed
my coats and taught me to sew
–H. M. Z.

In loving memory of my mum and the
many dresses she sewed, knitted, and
crocheted for me when I was a child
–L. M.

Text copyright © 2009 by Harriet Ziefert
Illustrations copyright © 2009 by Liz Murphy
All rights reserved / CIP Data is available.
Published in the United States 2009 by
🍎 Blue Apple Books
515 Valley Street, Maplewood, NJ 07040
www.blueapplebooks.com
Distributed in the U.S. by Chronicle Books
First Edition
Printed in China
ISBN: 978-1-934706-45-9

1 3 5 7 9 10 8 6 4 2

My grandma is good at sewing. Every year she makes me a special dress.

Grandma has stacks of material.
It's hard to choose, so Grandma helps me find two
fabrics that I like and says she will use them both.

Then Grandma takes my measurements.
She measures from the back of my neck to my waist;
from my waist to my knees; all around my waist;
and all around my chest.

I tell Grandma she's
tickling my toes.

Grandma answers, "Stay still for just two more minutes,
then we'll start your dress."

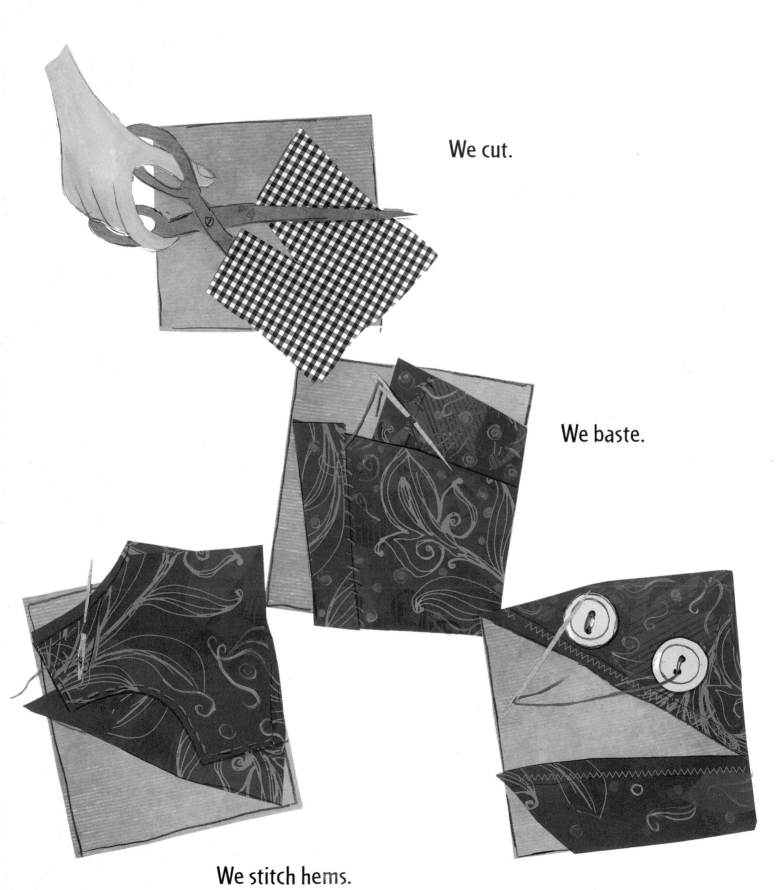

We cut.

We baste.

We stitch hems.

We sew on buttons.

Sometimes Grandma lets me press the power button on the sewing machine with my foot.

When it's time for me to say good-bye,
Grandma promises to work on my dress
and have it ready soon.

Just look at my present from Grandma.
A one-of-a-kind party dress!
I can't wait to try it on.

"Pretty as a princess!"
says Grandma.

"A perfect fit!"
says Mommy.

"Thank you,
Grandma!"

Here I am at my little cousin's birthday party.

How do I look?

The next year, when I am seven, Grandma talks to me about saving the earth.

"We all need to do our part," she says. "We should use new material only if we have to. You're no wider, just taller, so let's start with what we have and add to it."

"Grandma, I like to wear short dresses with leggings. Can you make me pink leggings?"

"Good idea," says Grandma. "I have some pink stretch material which will be perfect."

Here I am in last year's dress . . .

with pink leggings . . .

and a new pair of shoes.

I've put on a green belt
to match my shoes.

How do I look?

Now I am eight.

Grandma offers to make me a new dress,
but I don't really want one.

I like my old dress. It's comfy and I want
to wear it some more. And I like helping
the environment.

Grandma has an idea.
She says, "Let's recycle. I'll take this dress apart.
Then I'll reuse all the fabric and make something
new and different."

"We won't waste, Grandma, will we?"

"No, dear, we won't waste anything."

Grandma uses a special
ripping tool.

In less than an hour my old
dress is in pieces:

belt . . .

bodice . . .

skirt . . .

slip . . .

zipper . . .

and
buttons.

Grandma decides to make me a
sleeveless jumper. She says I can
wear it with or without a shirt.
She also promises to knit a
sweater to cover my arms,
so I won't be cold in winter.

"Grandma, does knitting save
the environment?" I ask.

"Yes," she answers. "I don't have
to use the sewing machine. And
I have four skeins of wool I've
been wanting to use for a long,
long time."

Here I am in my recycled dress.
And my knitted cardigan.

How do I look?

I wear the dress to lots of birthday parties–including my own.

I tell my friends, "This is my forever dress. I've worn it forever . . . well, almost forever. Since I was six."

Now I am nearly ten. My shape is
changing. I am growing all around.
I ask Grandma to measure me for
a new dress.

Grandma doesn't have to say,
"Don't wiggle," or "Stand still."
I'm a big kid now.

I'm going to recycle my old dress.
I'll give it to my little cousin.
For awhile, it can be her
forever dress.

Here I am in my big kid outfit.

I like the patterns.

And the colors.

Blue is my new favorite.

How do I look?

The End